G.I. DOGS

HERO PUP
OF WORLD WAR I

SGT. STUBBY

Other books by
LAURIE CALKHOVEN

G.I. Dogs:
Judy, Prisoner of War

Military Animals

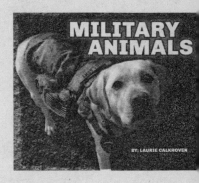

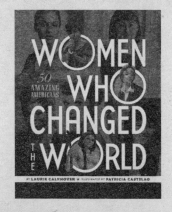

Women Who
Changed the World

G.I. DOGS

HERO PUP
OF WORLD WAR I

SGT
STUBBY

Laurie Calkhoven

Scholastic Inc.

Copyright © 2018 by Laurie Calkhoven

All rights reserved. Published by Scholastic Inc., *Publishers since 1920*. SCHOLASTIC and associated logos are trademarks and/or registered trademarks of Scholastic Inc.

The publisher does not have any control over and does not assume any responsibility for author or third-party websites or their content.

No part of this publication may be reproduced, stored in a retrieval system, or transmitted in any form or by any means, electronic, mechanical, photocopying, recording, or otherwise, without written permission of the publisher. For information regarding permission, write to Scholastic Inc., Attention: Permissions Department, 557 Broadway, New York, NY 10012.

While inspired by real events and historical characters, this is a work of fiction and does not claim to be historically accurate or portray factual events or relationships. Please keep in mind that references to actual persons, living or dead, business establishments, events, or locales may not be factually accurate, but rather fictionalized by the author.

Library of Congress Cataloging-in-Publication Data available

ISBN 978-1-338-18525-6

10 9 8 7 6 5 4 3   18 19 20 21 22

Printed in the U.S.A.   40
First edition, September 2018

Book design by Baily Crawford

For Becky,

with love and gratitude

PROLOGUE

GERMAN SPY!

A dense fog covered the battlefield. This was the day my unit was supposed to recapture the French town of Marchéville from the Germans, but until the fog lifted the men rested. My human, Bob Conroy, was sleeping, so I left him to go on patrol.

I padded through my unit, making sure all was well. Shadowy figures moved through the fog. Even the sounds they made were hazy and muffled. As always, my ears listened for the screams of German bombs and my nose was on alert for a whiff of poison gas. If I had learned nothing else since I arrived on the battlefield in France with the US Army's 26th Yankee Division in February

1918, it was to avoid poison gas. My nose smelled it long before the men's did, so my guys counted on me to warn them when the gas was on its way.

This morning everything seemed fine. The men rested, getting ready for their big push as soon as the order to attack came from headquarters. A few of them needed me to remind them that everything was going to be all right, but most of them were calm and waiting.

The fog lifted just for a moment, and that's when I saw a man wandering around. He was making marks on paper and checking everything out as if he had never seen it before.

Something's wrong, I thought.

Then I noticed that he wasn't wearing the khaki uniform of an American doughboy. I recognized that gray uniform. He was German, and Germans were the enemy.

A low growl rose in my throat as I moved toward him. He could only be trouble, and I wasn't going to let him get near my guys.

The German soldier quickly shoved his papers in his

jacket and reached out as if to pet me. He whispered what must have been German for, "C'mere, boy."

I'm too smart to fall for your tricks. You're not my friend.

I didn't take my eyes off him. I barked to alert the guys that there was a problem. *German enemy in our midst! Hurry!*

The German's eyes widened. He could see I meant business. He turned on his heel and started to run, but no soldier can run faster than me. With one last bark, I leaped and planted my teeth in his backside, getting a mouthful of gray serge material.

The German was facedown in the mud, struggling to get free. I kept my jaw clamped shut, and I heard his pants begin to rip as he tried to pull away. I growled a warning.

Don't try it, buddy. You won't make it. But really I was thinking, *Help! I can't hold on forever.*

Luckily, my barking had done the trick. Three American G.I.s ran up to us, and I knew it was safe to let go. They pulled the man to his feet.

"*Kamerad,*" he said. "*Kamerad.*"

But of course he wasn't a *kamerad*, which means "friend." He was the enemy.

"Surrender," he said in English. "Surrender."

I growled again. Lots of German soldiers had surrendered, and none of them had snuck around making marks on paper.

One of my guys reached into the man's jacket and pulled out the papers.

"You're not here to surrender, *kamerad*," the G.I. said. "You were drawing a map of our positions."

The German looked scared.

"Hey, Stubby, you caught a spy," one of the other G.I.s said.

"A spy? Stubby caught a spy!" another guy yelled. He was loud enough for the men nearby to hear, but not loud enough to draw German fire.

Then my human, Bob, ran over to find out what was going on, and everyone started making a huge fuss, which was kind of nice, even though I was just doing my job. By the rules of war, any valuables the prisoner had belonged to me, including the Iron Cross he wore on his uniform.

The Iron Cross is one of the highest honors a German soldier can achieve, and now—while the other guys marched the prisoner to headquarters—Bob pinned that cross to the coat I wore.

Even better, the company cook threw me a juicy bone!

The capture of that German spy would get me unofficially promoted to sergeant, the only dog sergeant in the entire US Army.

But we didn't celebrate my promotion for long. I had to hide the bone and hope the enormous rats that ran around in the trenches wouldn't find it before I got back. The fog was lifting, and it was time to head into battle.

But before I can tell you about that, I have to tell you about how I was lost and alone on the streets of New Haven, Connecticut, joined the army, and found a special human. Then I traveled all the way to France to help win what people called the Great War.

This is my story, and I promise it's amazing.

CHAPTER 1

YOU'RE IN THE ARMY NOW

The first thing you have to know about me is that I don't remember much from before I joined the army. I don't remember my mom or how I came to live on the streets of New Haven. The first thing I remember is prowling around by myself looking for food.

I know I started out with a human owner because of my tail. I'm what most people call a Boston bull terrier or just a plain old Boston terrier. Or mostly, anyway. Like a lot of dogs, I'm more than one breed. But mostly, I'm a bull terrier. One of the things that makes Boston terriers stand out is our tails. Our tails are shortened a couple of days after we're born to make sure we're especially stylish. And I'm no exception, especially when it comes to style.

People used the words "brindle-patterned" to describe me. My face and paws were mostly white, but the rest of me was a kind of stripy brown. Like I said, *stylish*.

I was too young to remember my early days or what came next. I just know I landed on the streets of New Haven. I'm smart and strong and flat-out handsome (not to mention charming), so I did all right. Sometimes I palled around with other dogs, but mostly I was on my own. I quickly learned that the garbage cans in alleys behind restaurants were the best places to find food— second only to those behind butcher shops. One nice butcher used to save bones for me (did I mention that I'm charming?). When I was really lucky, some of those bones had meat on them.

I had a few favorite places where I curled up to sleep— places where I was well hidden. It was hard to stay warm and dry in the winter, though.

Life was okay, but I sometimes came across dogs that belonged to humans. They always had enough food to eat and a warm place to sleep. Plus, they got scratched in places that I couldn't reach with my paws. As much as I loved my life, I knew it could be better if I had a human of my own.

Then the United States declared war, and I got my chance.

The world had been at war for three years by then. France, Great Britain, and Russia (known as the Allied powers) were fighting with Germany and Austria-Hungary (the Central powers).

Soon lots of other countries joined in on one side or another. Today people call this conflict World War I, but back then it was simply known as the Great War. Great not because it was awesome, but because it was so huge.

Three years after it all started, the two armies were still fighting it out in the trenches of France, and it didn't seem like anyone was ever going to win.

That's when Germany started attacking supply ships from other countries, including ours. And then they tried to talk Mexico into going to war against us in exchange for land in the American Southwest.

The United States had stayed out of the conflict for as long as possible, but that did it. President Woodrow Wilson was forced to declare war on Germany on April 6, 1917. The United States joined Great Britain, France, and Russia and became one of the Allies.

The only reason why I know all that is because the army came to New Haven a couple of months after President Wilson declared war. New England's soldiers started showing up at Yale University to train on the athletic fields.

Now ask yourself—what do soldiers need more than anything?

You might think discipline. You might think gun training. Both of those things are true. But the first answer I came up with was food, and lots of it. No more back alleys and garbage cans for me! All I had to do was follow my nose. Not only did I find lots and lots of food, I found a bunch of humans that were away from home, lonely, and in need of good company.

What could be better at a time like that than the good company of a cheerful, friendly, handsome charmer like myself?

It wasn't long before the men—or doughboys as the American soldiers were called—got to know me. Not only did the cooks save me bones and other scraps, the doughboys did, too. The men named me Stubby after my shortened tail, and I learned to run to whoever said my name. It usually meant food. Or a good scratch. Or both.

It also wasn't long before I picked out my very favorite human. His name was James Robert Conroy, and everyone called him Bob. He was from Connecticut.

It happened like this: One day I was running through camp when I heard a whistle. I looked up to see a friendly face with a wide smile.

"Who do we have here?" he asked, reaching down to scratch me behind my ears—one of my three favorite places to be scratched (my belly and under my chin being the other two).

"That's Stubby," another soldier answered. "Haven't you met him yet?"

"Hey, there, Stubby," Bob said. "Pleased to meet'cha."

Now he scratched my second favorite place to be scratched, followed by my third.

I think you're my favorite human, I thought.

It wasn't just that Bob knew exactly where to scratch me, or that he started sharing every single meal with me. Or even that I slept next to him on his cot and he didn't mind a bit. Bob smelled the way the very best humans smell—kind, friendly, and loving. I continued to visit my other friends in camp—especially the cooks—but Bob and I became best buddies. When his sisters came to visit at the end of the summer, I was the first friend he introduced them to.

I wasn't just an eating machine, either. I was a soldier. When the soldiers marched, I marched alongside them, no matter how far they went. When they practiced digging trenches, I inspected their work. When they learned to shoot rifles, I barked encouragement. I even stood guard with Bob when it was his turn and kept my ears peeled for enemies.

There were bugle calls for everything. The day began

with reveille at daybreak and ended with taps as the sun went down. In between, there were bugle calls to assemble on the field, bugle calls to start marching, to stop marching, and everything else you can think of. My favorites were the bugle calls that let the men know it was time to eat.

I learned all the bugle calls. I even paraded next to the men while they marched in formation.

Bob taught me one trick that was everyone's favorite. The men spent a lot of time every day saluting. All that touching your hand to your forehead when you didn't even have to scratch seemed silly to me, but I wanted to do anything Bob did.

He taught me to sit and then rise up on my back legs before I brought my right front paw to my forehead. The real trick was to wait until the other person saluted me back, and then I could drop down to all fours again.

I don't know why the men made such a fuss over a silly little trick, but they had me do it over and over again.

So life was good. Lots and lots of food, any number of

soldiers who'd let me hop on their bunks to sleep, and a special human who made me his.

There was just one problem. We were in Connecticut and the war was in France. At some point, my human was going to have to ship out, and dogs weren't allowed.

Bob had to find a way to get me to France.

CHAPTER 2

STOWAWAY

One day in the middle of September, Bob and his regiment started to take down their tents and pack up their gear.

That night, wearing heavy backpacks, the bugle called for the men to assemble near the football stadium's gates. Then they began to march.

As always, I marched alongside them. I heard my name now and again, but the men weren't talking to me. They were asking Bob what was going to happen.

"I don't know," he told them, over and over again. "I guess Stubby will stand by us for as long as he can."

That's exactly what I'll do, I thought. *No one's going to separate Bob and me if I have anything to say about it.*

When the soldiers boarded a railroad car at the train station, so did I. No one tried to stop me.

We rode all night. I curled up on Bob's lap for a nap, and he and a couple of other men propped up their gear to hide me from the officers. In the morning, we stopped at Newport News, Virginia.

Bob looked right into my eyes before we got off the train. His were sadder than I had ever seen them, even when he said goodbye to his sisters in camp.

"I'm afraid this is the end of the line, Stubby," he said. "They don't let dogs on troopships."

I looked right back at him and raised my chin. *You're going to have to find a way, because I'm not leaving you.*

Bob didn't say anything, but I guess he got the message. When the men marched toward the port, I marched right at their sides. People lined up, waving and cheering them on. Some of them pointed at me. It made them happy to see me heading to Europe with the soldiers. Couldn't the army see how important I was, too?

We neared a giant ship—the SS *Minnesota*—and I gave Bob a quiet bark. *Look at that huge ship. There's plenty of room for a dog to hide.*

Bob understood. While the doughboys were milling around on the dock waiting to board the ship, he and one of his friends introduced themselves to a sailor and shared the problem. It wasn't long before they had a plan. While Bob and the other doughboys marched on board the *Minnesota* under the eyes of their officers, the sailor wrapped me in a blanket and carried me up the gangplank. No one noticed.

I hid out in a coal bin in the engine room. It was dark and dusty and noisy. I admit, I was a little scared, but I knew if I was going to be reunited with Bob, I'd have to be quiet. And so I was. The big ship swayed in the waves of the harbor as it pulled out of port and I thought I might be sick, but as the ship gained speed, my stomach settled down. Now it was just a matter of waiting—waiting until we were far enough out to sea that no one would try to put me in a lifeboat and send me back to shore. I spent two whole days in that coal bin. The sailor who hid me came by with food and water, but it felt long and lonely. Then, finally, it was safe to come out.

I was so happy to run again that I dashed up and down the length of the engine room a bunch of times. When I got that out of my system, I barked at the sailor.

Take me to my human. Take me to see Bob.

And he did.

Bob scratched me in all my favorite places while I licked his face. Even though my nose was full of coal dust, he smelled just like I remembered.

"Oh boy, are you dirty," he said.

I couldn't see myself, but when he pulled his hands away, they were covered in black dust. Personally, I don't mind a little dirt, but even I could tell I needed a bath.

Bob carried me downstairs to what the sailors and soldiers called the head and gave me a good scrubbing. It wasn't long before I was back to my regular old, handsome self.

When we finished, Bob took me to see the guys. "But

if any officers come around, make yourself scarce," he warned.

We trotted into a big room filled with bunk after bunk after bunk.

"Stubby's back!" someone said.

"Yay, Stubby! You broke out of the brig," another added.

"Brig" is the navy's word for jail, and I guess I sort of was in jail for a while.

Boy am I glad to be free! I barked.

There were whistles and cheers. Everyone was as happy to see me as I was to see them. I made the rounds, sniffing and licking my favorites. More than one of my soldiers had a special treat stashed away for me, which I happily accepted.

Once I had greeted my old friends, Bob took me on a tour of the ship so I could make new ones. Up on deck, I got my first look at the ocean, and let me tell you, it was big. I barked a hello to the sentries who were searching the waters for German submarines, or U-boats, and to the guys down in the engine room.

You won't be surprised to learn that my very favorite spot on the whole ship was the mess hall—the place where the guys gathered to eat—and the kitchen just behind it. I was at my most charming when I met the cooks. The guys complained about the way the food tasted sometimes, but I never did. Those cooks worked *hard*, and they saved the best scraps for me.

As long as I stayed away from the officers' areas, I pretty much had the full run of the ship for the time it took to cross the Atlantic Ocean—almost a whole month. I visited the sentries, played ball games on deck, and when I needed a nap, there was always a soldier to snuggle up against while he read or wrote letters home. At night, I slept next to Bob, the most comfortable place in the world.

Some guys in the machine shop were nice enough to make me a set of dog tags for my collar that matched the ones the soldiers wore. Mine read:

STUBBY

102nd INF

26th DIV

The 102nd was Bob's infantry regiment, which was just one regiment in the 26th Yankee Division. The tags also included the name *J. R. Conroy* and Bob's service number to make sure everyone knew who I belonged to.

Like Bob said, whenever I saw an officer, I made myself scarce. It made no sense at all, but Bob seemed to think that the officers didn't like dogs. He was convinced they would make him give me away if they found me.

Whenever I had a close call and saw him worrying, I looked right into his eyes.

No one is going to separate us—not ever.

It took about a month to sail all the way to Saint-Nazaire, France. And I didn't get caught. It was October when we spotted land in the distance.

The men and I gathered on deck for our first look at France.

"It looks so peaceful," Bob said. "No sign of war from here."

One of the other doughboys slapped him on the back. "We'll bring peace back," he said. "Just give us a couple of months, and we'll have those Germans on the run."

On our last day at sea, I made the rounds saying good-bye to the cooks and my favorite sailors on the SS *Minnesota* before we disembarked.

Watch out for U-boats, and thanks for all the soup bones, I told them. *I hope the food is just as good in France.*

When it was time, Bob wrapped me in his coat and asked his buddies to create a distraction. They joked and laughed in really loud voices while they jostled each other around on the gangplank. All eyes turned to them, and Bob and I made it to land unseen.

Let me tell you, walking on land after being on the ocean for almost four weeks was very strange. It felt like the ground was rising and falling like the ocean waves, even though it really wasn't. It took me a while to get my land legs.

I was still working on that when one of the 26th Division's top brass spotted us, and I guess he recognized me from Connecticut. Before we knew it, he had marched up behind us.

"Soldier," he demanded. "Want to explain why you brought a dog to war?"

Everyone around us got quiet, waiting to see what the officer was going to do. Was he going to report us to Major General Clarence "Daddy" Edwards, the head of the whole division?

Don't even think about trying to send me home, I thought.

I could tell by the look on Bob's face that he was scared. He spun on his heels and saluted.

I knew what that meant. I sat down, leaned back, and raised my right paw to my forehead. I held it there for a long time.

C'mon, Officer, you're supposed to salute back. Don't you know the rules?

The officer looked surprised, and then finally did his job and saluted the two of us back.

I dropped down to all fours again, but Bob stayed at attention. "He followed us onto the ship, sir. Stubby wants to fight the Germans, too."

The officer shook his head and sighed. "The dog can stay on as a mascot," he barked, "but make sure he never gets in the way of the work of this army."

"Yes, sir," Bob told him. "Stubby's a good dog, sir."

The officer stomped away, and Bob breathed a big sigh of relief.

"Hear that, Stubby? You're our official mascot. No one can make you go away now."

CHAPTER 3

GAS ATTACK

The 102nd Infantry, part of the 26th Yankee Division, was among the first troops to reach France. The French people were happy to see us, but we had to wait for more US doughboys to arrive before we could enter the fight.

We didn't stay in Saint-Nazaire for long. Almost as soon as the commanding officer said I could stick around, we were on the march to another train station. We piled onto trains and spent a few days traveling inland in cramped, uncomfortable railroad cars designed for freight, not people.

We finally arrived at a place called Neufchâteau and were able to stretch our legs. The town didn't have enough room for all of us. Officers had real beds in a hotel, but the rest of us had to make do. Bob and I were lucky enough to be assigned to a drafty barn on the outskirts of town. It was cold at night, but we had each other to snuggle up with. That made it cozy.

The army hadn't figured out how to set up kitchens and feed us all yet, so we headed to nearby storehouses for supplies, and my small group of guys took turns cooking in the barnyard. A lot of them complained about the food, but that just meant more for me. Sometimes we bought food at local farms and restaurants, and I often got to play with the children who gathered around whenever they spotted the American doughboys.

At night, when training ended, the guys would tell one another stories. Some asked what the others thought we'd face in battle, but mostly they talked about home. Some had wives and girlfriends and they'd show their pictures around, and all the other guys would whistle and say they were beauties and that the guys were lucky men.

Bob didn't have a sweetheart, but he did have sisters. He told stories about growing up with them. He even promised to introduce one of the other guys to his sisters when we all got home again.

By late October 1917, all of the Yankee Division had reached France, but we still needed more American soldiers before we could join the fight. While we waited, we did more training. Most of the fighting in France was done from trenches dug into the earth, and the men needed to practice fighting in them. They also learned how to fire machine guns and throw grenades. Let me tell you—that was LOUD. But I got used to it. And, of course, there was marching and marching and more marching.

French people, especially children, lined up to wave and cheer as the doughboys tramped by. I quickly became a favorite, of course. The children especially loved to run along beside me. I liked to stop and play with them, but I always ran after Bob again before he got too far away. I didn't know my way around France yet, and I didn't want to lose him.

The doughboys trained with one another, with the English—whom the men called Tommies—and with the French, known as *poilus*. I'm told that means "hairy," but the French men didn't seem to me to be any more hairy than the Americans. None of them had as much hair as a dog. I felt sorry for them about that. It meant they got cold a lot faster than I did.

Cold or not, furry or not, we all got ready to face our German enemies.

Bob was assigned to the 102nd's headquarters, and that meant I got assigned to headquarters, too. When he carried messages from one outfit to another, I trotted along next to his horse. We got to visit lots of towns, including one that made me a special medal in honor of Joan of Arc, a famous French heroine who led an army in another war a long, long time ago. I also stayed at Bob's side when he was on guard duty, keeping an eye out for enemy soldiers. But of course my favorite place to go with him, when it was finally set up, was the mess tent.

One thing we all hated was the mud. That fall, it rained almost every day, and the thick mud stuck to everything. It was almost a relief when the temperature dropped and the mud froze, but then we were marching in snow and sleet—even once in a blizzard. Our barn, which seemed so cozy when we first arrived, turned into one big icy draft. The men's boots fell apart. I started sleeping on top of Bob's feet to keep him from getting frostbite. The best gift he got that winter was a pair of woolen socks knitted by his sister.

We celebrated our first Christmas away from home. The cooks made a special meal, and the men all told one another that the war would be won and they'd be back home by the next Christmas.

I hope that's true, I thought. *I like home, especially now that I have a human. Where Bob goes, I go.*

In January 1918, the 102nd got a new commander. Major General "Daddy" Edwards was still in charge of the whole division, but Colonel John Henry "Gatling Gun" Parker took over the regiment. I made sure to win him over with my salute, and the men said I was the only member of the regiment who could talk back to him without being court-martialed or kicked out of the army.

It was Gatling Gun Parker who led us into the combat zone. On February 5, 1918, we took a position behind the French at a place called Chemin des Dames. The Germans were east of our position, and the French were just opposite them. Our job was to be ready if the Germans broke through the French front lines and to stop them from pushing on to Paris, the French capital. Everyone agreed it would be a disaster if the Germans reached Paris.

The front lines were a complicated series of interconnected trenches dug into the ground. The men moved between the front-line trenches and the underground living areas farther back. The best bunkers had wooden planks covering the walls and floors, and some had wooden bunk beds built into them, too. In others, the men slept in the dirt and mud.

In between the German and the Allied trenches was an open field called No Man's Land. No one wanted to get caught out there without the trenches for protection, let me tell you. I learned pretty quickly that it was best to stay underground. Whenever anyone or anything popped up above the trenches, the Germans fired their guns. The same thing happened if we made too much noise. Someone would laugh or shout and then—boom!—a shell would come our way.

Bob was assigned to the regiment's intelligence unit. Our job was to figure out enemy troop movements and report back to the top brass. That meant we moved around a lot in the trenches, talking to soldiers who knew what was going on. It was so cold that moving was mostly a good thing, and along the way I got to know a lot of the soldiers in the regiment. But there were lots of times when Bob was too close to the fighting. I didn't know how I'd keep him safe when that happened.

Sometimes there were enemy raids and the men had to fight almost face-to-face, but mostly the fighting came in the form of artillery fire. Pretty soon we all learned to tell the difference between the big French guns and the German guns just by the sounds they made.

I heard the shells coming long before the men did, and I tried to let them know when a shell was about to explode right in front of us. But the thing we all worried about the most was poison gas. All of the G.I.s had their own gas masks. Horses and dogs had them, too, and Bob got one for me. My French-made doggy mask didn't fit right, and Bob didn't think it would keep the bad air out. He and a

French lieutenant worked together to make one that would keep me safe. Then Bob made me practice wearing it over and over again.

In March, we experienced our first poison gas attack. I smelled something strange—something I had never smelled before. Then the bells rang to warn us, but it was too late. The gas shells were already filling the air with a smelly green haze. Bob and I didn't get our gas masks on in time. Hours later, when the shelling finally stopped, my eyes still burned and it was hard to breathe. Without my gas mask, I would have died. It was a whole day before I felt better.

You won't get me twice, I thought.

I learned my lesson. After that, I was on alert. I could smell that gas long before the humans did, so I created a warning system of my own. I ran through the trenches barking at the men until they put on their masks and rang the warning bells.

Once, when the battle was particularly loud and Bob couldn't hear me barking over the din, I nosed my mask into his hand and he got the message.

Another time, one of the soldiers, John Curtin, was sound asleep.

Wake up! I barked. *There's a gas shell coming.*

He didn't move.

I barked some more, but it had been days since he had gotten a decent rest and he didn't hear a thing. Finally, I jumped right on top of him and nipped his nose. That got his attention.

"Stubby, stop," he groaned. "I was dreaming about my girl back home."

Dream or no dream, he had to put his mask on. There was no time to lose. I shoved my nose under his blanket and nudged him until he finally figured out that he'd better pay attention. Then I nosed his gas mask.

You're not going to get gassed on my watch, I barked. *Put your mask on. And mine, too.*

Gas attack warnings weren't my only job on the front lines. While Bob was moving through the trenches gathering intelligence, I got to know the men. I could smell the ones who were the most afraid and needed some dog time to feel better. I reminded the men of home, and petting me calmed them down. You need to keep your wits about you on the battlefield, and you can't do that when you're out of your mind with fear.

It's also hard to keep your wits about you when you're covered in fleas and lice, and when rats are running all over and stealing your food. That was another job of mine—catching rats. I was a good hunter, but even I couldn't keep up with them. They grew to be as big as cats and weren't scared of humans at all. They ran over the men while they were sleeping and even tried to take food right out of their hands. Those rats were on a constant hunt for food. I guess that's why they were so big.

All of that great work I did made me popular—even with the French soldiers. One day, I decided it was time to check out French food. I was always hearing about how great it was supposed to be. So I wandered a bit farther away than usual to find a French mess tent.

I was just starting to get to know the cook—a nice guy who wasn't hairy at all—when one of those French soldiers decided he wanted to keep me around. First, he made sure the cook slipped me a generous sample of that night's stew. While I was busy judging for myself whether French food was better than American food, that *poilu* slipped a leash around my neck!

Hey, no fair! I barked. *I need to be free.*

I had always been able to roam wherever I wanted, and let me tell you, I did not like that leash one bit. I tried to run, but when he didn't have his hands on the leash, he tied me to the wall of his bunker.

Let me go! Bob must be worried about me, and I need to get back to my guys, I barked. *Read my dog tags!*

But the *poilu* didn't listen. It wasn't until a doughboy named Smitty spotted me and had a big argument with the French guy that I finally got away. Smitty walked me back to the 102nd's headquarters. When we got close, he took off that horrible leash. I couldn't wait to get back to Bob. As soon as I picked up his scent, I bounded in his direction.

"Stubby!" Bob shouted. "Where've you been?"

Smitty explained what had happened, and I snuggled up next to my guy while he scratched me in all my favorite places.

No more leashes for me, I told him. *I do not like being tied up. And by the way, French cooking isn't any better than ours.*

That problem was solved, but we were about to face a much bigger one.

During those early months on the front lines, we shadowed the French soldiers and learned what we could from them. We learned what it meant to live and fight in the trenches, but we hadn't participated in any big battles.

That was about to change.

CHAPTER 4

WOUNDED

In the spring, the Germans put on a new offensive and our training came to an end. It was time to fight for real. The Yankee Division was moved to the town of Toul, where we had to defend our territory without the help of the French. Headquarters was set up in a small village just north of Toul called Beaumont, but Bob and I were practically on the front lines.

We tried to take our new position quietly, but the Germans weren't fooled. Across the shell-pocked stretch of No Man's Land, the men could see German signs that read, *Welcome, 26th Division.*

It wasn't just signs that "welcomed" us, either. German gas and artillery shells rained down on us along with real rain, filling our trenches with puddles and mud. We answered with artillery shells of our own. The noise didn't stop.

In the early morning hours of April 20, 1918, the Germans attacked with more than just shells and bullets. Enemy storm troopers, soldiers specially trained in hand-to-hand combat, appeared out of nowhere and rushed our front line. Our men tried to hold them back, but we were outnumbered six to one.

The storm troopers overran the first trench and then advanced to the next. All the American soldiers joined the battle. Radio communication had been cut off by German shells, but runners arrived at headquarters with news of the attack. Bob grabbed his gun, and we headed out to the trenches to help the doughboys while others prepared to retreat with any important papers that couldn't fall into enemy hands. Even the company cook jumped into the trenches and started swinging his meat cleaver at the German soldiers!

Many of our men were killed. Many others had been taken prisoner in the storm troopers' first assault. Those of us who were left did all we could to make sure the Germans didn't gain any more ground. The shelling and gunfire continued for hours.

Finally, in late afternoon, the storm troopers began to retreat back to their own lines. The battle quieted and then it seemed to be over. I jumped out of the trench to check things out. I thought there might be wounded men who needed my help.

Big mistake.

I had just started to nose around when a shell we all thought was a dud suddenly exploded, sending shrapnel flying in all directions.

A piece of fiery metal hit me in the chest. It hurt so much that I couldn't move. All I could do was howl.

I picked out Bob's voice under all the other battle-field noises. "Don't move, Stubby," he yelled. "I'm coming for you."

Don't worry; I'm not going anywhere.

Bob waited until things got quiet again. Then he

crawled out of the trench and slithered toward me on his belly.

Be careful, I whimpered. *Keep your head down.*

Bob wrapped his arms around me and pressed against my wound. It hurt, but I knew he was trying to stop the flow of blood. Then he slithered back toward the trench with me in his arms. He handed me over to a pair of waiting hands, and then he fell back into the trench after me.

Whew! We made it.

But I still wasn't out of danger. My wound was bad, even I could see that. Bob did his best to clean it up and stop me from losing too much blood, but I needed more help than he could give me.

Bob made his way back toward headquarters with me in his arms and stopped at a first aid station.

A medic checked me out. I tried not to whimper because I wanted to be brave for Bob and my other guys. But boy did that hurt!

"How bad is it, Doc?" Bob asked. His forehead was creased with worry.

"It's a serious wound," the doctor said, "but with rest, Stubby will recover."

Then he told Bob that I'd have to go to a field hospital for help. I needed stitches, and I needed to be away from the noise and the mud and the cold. Bob laid me down in an ambulance next to a wounded soldier.

"You get well, Stubby," he said. "I'll come and visit you as soon as I can."

I took a last look at Bob. *Stay alive, my friend. I'm coming back*, I wanted to tell him. *We'll be together again soon.*

The first few days in the field hospital were a blur. A surgeon put me to sleep before cleaning my wound and stitching it up. Then someone else put bandages on me. They strapped me to a cot so I wouldn't move around and damage their work.

Don't worry, I thought. *It hurts too much to move.*

Every day, someone cleaned my wound and gave me new bandages. And each day, my wound hurt a little less. Pretty soon, I was awake more than I was asleep, and I was eating and drinking like I normally did. I knew my guys at the front would be really sad until I came back, but I took full advantage of the quiet and the rest at the hospital to get strong again.

As soon as I could, I started visiting the other wounded soldiers in their hospital beds. Some were in pain, some were scared, and some just needed a reminder of home. I made them all feel better.

If I can make it, you can, too, I told them. *Get better.*

I was glad to be doing such important work, but I could sometimes hear the big guns in the distance, and I knew my place was by Bob's side. I needed to get back to him. I needed to protect him.

I had been at the hospital for almost six weeks when I realized I didn't have any more pain—not even a little twinge where my stitches had been. I experimented by jumping up on one of the soldier's beds, and I felt completely fine. I could run just like I could before my injury, too. I had a small scar, but otherwise I was back to normal.

I jumped around to show the doctors and nurses that I was completely healed.

Hey, Doc, I'm all better! I need to get back to Bob and to the war, I told my surgeon.

He understood. Just two days later, I hitched a ride with a couple of soldiers who were on their way back to the front. I was way more excited than they were. They didn't have a Bob of their own to get back to.

It was early June when I returned to the front lines. What had come to be called the Battle of Seicheprey had been over for more than a month. The Yankee Division must have scared those Germans good—the cook waving his meat cleaver around was enough to give anyone nightmares—because they had been pretty quiet since I left for the hospital. There certainly weren't any more visits from the storm troopers while I was away.

The men sure were glad to have me back, especially Bob. We had a good long visit with scratching and licking and hugging—and even a few delicious treats—when I arrived. Everyone was thrilled to see me in fighting shape again.

Even better, spring had given way to summer. Not only was it warm, the mud had mostly dried up. The trenches were still full of rats—I got on that job pretty quick, let me tell you—and the men were still covered in fleas and lice, but compared to March and April, life was good.

The war hadn't disappeared completely, though. Shells still flew, and there were a few German raids across No Man's Land, but nothing like the offensive in which I was injured. Our guys were able to defend against every single German attack. More and more American doughboys were arriving in France all the time, and slowly the Allies began to regain territory that had earlier been lost to the enemy.

During that time, Bob and I traveled through the trenches, delivering messages and collecting information about German troop movements. We kept our heads down and stayed underground as much as we could, but more than once, we had a close call with a bullet or a shell.

Rumors began to fly that our regiment was going to get a break. The men had been fighting for nearly five months, and they thought it was time for a rest.

They were dreaming of visits to Paris, and some said we would march in a Fourth of July parade right past the Eiffel Tower.

We all thought that rumor was coming true when we were ordered out of the trenches. No one told us where we were going, as the army couldn't risk men talking to one another about their plans in front of German spies by mistake. So we were full of hope as piled into the train cars. Every town we passed through was full of French people waving and cheering. I barked back at them and Bob and all the guys yelled. It was like a big party. We were pushing back the Germans. Everyone was hopeful that the war would end soon.

This is great! I thought. *No more bullets flying at us and lots of happy people!*

There was a huge cheer when the men spotted the Eiffel Tower in the distance.

"I told you we were going to Paris!" one of them shouted.

The men were still whistling and cheering when the

train shifted to another set of railroad tracks and made a turn.

Suddenly, there was silence. We weren't going to Paris.

We passed more towns after that, and the French people came out to wave and cheer for us like before. Only now the men didn't cheer back.

We're going back to war, I realized.

CHAPTER 5

THE MARNE

It turns out that the Germans were trying to push through Allied lines in another front-line sector of France: the Marne. There had been a big battle in that part of France early in the war, and now there would be the Second Battle of the Marne.

If the Germans made their way through the Allied defenses there, they'd be in Paris, France's capital, in no time. The Allies were giving everything they had to make sure that didn't happen, and they needed the help of the Yankee Division.

We had barely arrived and taken a position outside the town of Château-Thierry on July 15, when the Germans put on a big push. We fought hard, and by July 17, they gave up their assault, but the battle wasn't over. Now it was our turn—the French and Americans fought together to regain territory from the enemy and send those Germans packing. The British and the Italians helped, too. It wasn't long before the Germans were in retreat.

Bob and I did our best to keep track of the German retreat and get that information back to headquarters. Sometimes we went to headquarters ourselves. Other times we sent messengers. Things were changing all the time. It was hard to keep up.

The Allies left the trenches behind, fighting and chasing the Germans through wheat fields. Night and day, day and night, the Allies pushed on. Without the cover of the trenches, our casualties mounted. As men were hit, they were hidden by the waist-high wheat.

That's when I took on a new job—finding wounded Americans and letting the medics know where they were. I could tell the difference between one of my guys and the enemy. They wore different uniforms and they talked differently. I had to pass the Germans right by. There were too many wounded Americans, and my guys came first—always.

I'd bark to let the medics know that I found someone who needed their help, and I'd stick around until they arrived.

Sometimes the doughboys were beyond saving. At first, I wanted to stop and give a proper goodbye to each one, but there were just too many. I learned to focus on the doughboys I could actually help.

The saddest were the ones who were still alive, but knew they wouldn't make it. I'd snuggle up next to them for their final moments so that they wouldn't be alone. Some of them thought I was their dog from back home, and it made me feel proud that I could bring them comfort in the end.

That's the shape Smitty was in when I found him in the wheat. Smitty had saved me from the French soldier with the awful leash. Smitty helped me get back to my Bob. I wish I could have saved him from this. I wish I could have helped him get back to his own family. But I couldn't.

At first look, I thought he might already be gone, but when I licked his cheek, his eyes fluttered and he focused on me just for a second. He tried to raise his arm to pet me, but he was too weak.

"Hey, Stubby," he whispered.

I ignored the blood and snuggled up next to him. His eyes fluttered again when I rested my nose on his shoulder. One tear slipped down his cheek. And then he was gone.

Goodbye, friend, I thought. *Thank you for saving me.*

I would have liked to have stayed with him until someone came to collect him for burial, but there were medics who needed my help to find the men who could still be saved.

If only Smitty could have hung on for a little while longer. Everyone said the war would be over any day. Germany was vowing to fight on, but it seemed like most of the German soldiers couldn't wait to surrender.

We collected lots of German prisoners. I was happy that they weren't going to be able to shoot at us anymore, but I didn't trust them. Bob used a translator to talk to some of them to learn more about German troop movements before they were marched to headquarters and then on to a prisoner of war camp.

I made sure to bark my meanest bark as they marched by. If anyone slipped out of line, I went after him. There would be no escaping when I was around.

Eyes straight ahead, prisoner, I'd bark. *No one escapes on my watch!*

By the time the Second Battle of the Marne was over in early August 1918, the Americans had lost fifty thousand men. We had taken eleven miles of territory back from the Germans, including woods, fields, and even a couple of towns. It was clear that Germany was losing the war. They knew it and we knew it. I just hoped they'd surrender fast before any more of my guys got hurt.

Bob and I were still in the small town of Château-Thierry when the battle ended. The people of the town were finally free of the Germans after years of occupation, and boy were they happy. We were all celebrating when I smelled a gas attack on the way.

I barked and barked. *Gas is coming! Poison gas!*

It was my special gas bark, and Bob knew exactly

what to do. He made sure the army rang the alarm bells and we all—soldiers, citizens, and dogs—got our gas masks on in time.

If the people of Château-Thierry weren't already grateful to us, they sure were now. They were so happy that they made me a uniform of my very own. It was a soft, tan leather and was even nicer than Bob's. There was gold braid stitched onto it along with my name and unit. There were official Yankee Division patches and an embroidered wreath of flags from every Allied country.

I still say fur is better than clothes any day, but I was proud of my coat. It made me the most stylish dog in the army, and I got it just in time to go to Paris on leave with Bob.

Everyone said Paris was the fashion capital of the world. Now that I had my uniform, I was ready to show those Parisian dogs just how fashionable a Boston terrier could be.

I worried all the way to Paris that we would get close enough to smell it and then be called back to the war again. But that didn't happen this time. Bob and I had ten whole days in the city—away from bombs, away from poison gas, away from war.

Ooh la la!

And let me tell you, the people of Paris love dogs! Bob had no trouble finding a hotel that would let me stay with him, and we had a swell time in all the outdoor cafés. Waiters made sure to bring me my very own water bowl, and Bob shared whatever food he ordered with me.

Wherever we went, I attracted a lot of attention. No one had ever seen a dog in uniform before, and Bob made sure to tell anyone who spoke English all about my work for the doughboys.

My special favorites were the youngest humans. Bob and I were checking out the Arc de Triomphe, a famous French monument, when two sisters came over to pet me instead of crossing the street like they intended. We didn't speak the same language, but we had a good visit, anyway, with some very nice scratching.

Then the girls said *au revoir,* which I knew meant "goodbye." They were just about to step off the curb when I heard a horse coming—fast.

Wait! Don't go! I barked. *A runaway horse!*

I ran in front of the girls and kept them on the side-walk. They thought I was trying to get some more pets and scratches in, but a split second later, a horse charged up the street with a crazy look in its eyes. Something must have spooked it, and it ran without seeing what was right in front of it. My new friends would have been tram-pled if it weren't for me.

The younger sister dropped to her knees and gave me a huge hug, while the older sister kept saying *"merci"* over and over again. That means "thank you."

"Je t'aime, Stubby," the younger one added. "I love you."

Happy to help, I barked. *Be safe!*

People who saw what happened called me a hero, and I guess maybe I was. But I sure was looking forward to a world where I didn't have to keep my friends from being shot, or gassed, or trampled. Peace couldn't come soon enough for me or for Bob. We had beaten the Germans at the Marne, but they still held other parts of France, and we had to go back to war and shake them loose.

CHAPTER 6

THE FINAL PUSH

When we got back to headquarters after our Paris vacation, Bob and I learned that the 102nd had another new commanding officer. Gatling Gun Parker was replaced by "Hiking Hiram" Bearss.

"Don't forget to impress him, Stubby," Bob whispered.

Don't worry, I thought. *I'll charm the new guy in no time.*

And I did. All it took was that salute Bob taught me back in Connecticut and I immediately won officers over. Hiking Hiram was no exception. I was irresistible.

Hiking Hiram led us on our next mission. We'd had the Germans on the run for weeks, and everyone knew they were going to lose the war, but they refused to give up. Our new mission was to regain territory in northeastern France that the Germans had won way back in 1914.

If we were going to win, we needed to have surprise on our side. The entire Yankee Division gathered in the dark of night in early September 1918 and began a ten-day march. Of course, most of the men didn't know where we were going. The army couldn't risk our plans getting back to German spies. We just knew we were on the march.

The men ate wild blackberries and cherries along the way. The cooks picked apples and fed us apple fritters. That helped make up for all the rain and the mud. If we weren't marching into battle, I think the men might have enjoyed their journey across France.

The French people sure appreciated us. Every time we marched through a town or a village, no matter how small or how damaged by the war, the people came out to cheer us on and to wish us luck.

Not surprisingly, they loved me, especially when I was wearing my uniform. I trotted along beside Bob looking as fierce and soldierlike as I could, but that didn't fool anyone. Children still ran beside me, laughing.

There were always cries of, *"Le chien! Le chien!"*—which means "dog" in French.

Things were pretty jolly until we were close to our objective, just south of the town of Verdun. The men got quieter and quieter, knowing what was in store. No one was looking forward to facing the German guns again.

Be safe everyone, I thought. At the same time, I knew that was impossible. Very soon I would have to say good-bye to more of my friends.

On the night of September 12, 1918, more than five hundred thousand American doughboys and one hundred thousand French *poilus* went on the attack. First, we hit the Germans with artillery fire, and in the morning, we advanced through fog and rain. We had the Germans on the run—they were giving up territory they had held for four years.

There were shells landing, bullets flying, and men

screaming. Throughout it all, Bob was busy trying to figure out the path of the Germans' retreat. We climbed hills whenever we could to try to spot them in the distance, and I worried every time that someone would send a shell in our direction, or a sniper would fire a bullet. We had a couple of close calls, but Bob and I stayed safe.

For four days, we seemed to be on the move almost constantly—marching through the night and taking territory during the day. The Germans had set a lot of fires on their retreat. The smoke burned our eyes and made the men cough as they raced forward. We captured prisoners and took possession of abandoned supplies and big guns along the way.

We were moving so quickly, our rolling kitchens couldn't keep up. The men were tired, hungry, and thirsty, but they kept advancing. After four days of hard fighting, we had cleared our area of Germans and freed the city of Saint-Mihiel.

The people of Saint-Mihiel were thrilled to see the last of the Germans. They hugged and kissed the tired, dirty doughboys as we marched through town. We were all so covered in mud that we were hardly recognizable, but I got my share of attention, too. I even got a nice bone for my troubles.

We didn't have time to celebrate before we got a new mission. Now we had to march through the never-ending rain, sixty miles north, to help in another operation. This one was designed to force Germany to surrender once and for all.

Leave it to the doughboys, I thought. *We'll get the job done.*

The top brass wanted us to take the Germans by surprise, but how could a force of more than half a million men, four thousand guns, and almost one hundred thousand horses on the march actually surprise anyone with ears—even inferior human ears? But soldiers have to follow orders, and so we did our best to be as quiet as half a million men could be. It took a couple of weeks of marching for us to take our new position.

The plan was to confuse the enemy with attacks on multiple fronts. The Yankee Division's job was to take two towns that were in German hands—Marchéville and Riaville—while other divisions fought a much larger battle nearby. That way, the Germans couldn't send all their soldiers to defend against the bigger battle.

On September 26, 1918, we were waiting for orders to begin our assault on Marchéville. I went on patrol to make sure all was well, and that's when I saw him—a German soldier lurking around and making marks on paper. This was no prisoner. And this guy wasn't here to surrender. He was a spy!

I barked to let my men know that something was wrong. I squared off in front of the guy and growled.

He tried to pretend he was a friend, but I knew better.

No spies on my watch, buddy!

When he saw that I meant business, he tried to run. But no soldier can run faster than me. I barked again to alert my guys to the danger and then leaped on the spy and sank my teeth into his pants. He fell facedown in the mud, and I held him there until help arrived.

That was when the guys promoted me to *Sergeant* Stubby, and it felt good. I even outranked Bob!

Whenever a German prisoner was captured, his

belongings were given to the doughboy who caught him. That's how I got the Iron Cross—one of the highest honors a German soldier can achieve.

"To the victor goes the spoils," one of the guys said. He unpinned the German's medal and handed it to Bob.

"Here you go, Stubby," Bob said. "I'll pin it in a place of honor."

And then he pinned it right over my backside. Everybody had a good laugh over that.

"That'll show the Kaiser what we think of him," some-one said.

The Kaiser, if you don't know, was the leader of Germany. He's one of the guys who started this whole big mess and made us all go to war.

The little medal ceremony was the end of our fun. That same day we got the order to attack, and attack we did. Everyone said we'd win this battle quickly and force Germany to surrender, but it dragged on and on. We lost too many men to shells and machine-gun fire. The replace-ments were young and scared and didn't have enough training. Sadly, many of them died the minute they reached the front.

You never knew when a German sniper was going to appear out of nowhere and take out a few of our guys before he disappeared again.

The offensive waged on, day after day. We all lost track of time. Bob didn't even look like himself anymore. I couldn't remember the last time he was able to take a shower, or shave, or put on a clean uniform. He didn't even have time to eat. I guess I looked just as ragged.

Some of our guys started to fall apart. I'd find them slumped somewhere, so tired and so frightened that they couldn't move. The rain hadn't stopped for days. The temperature was dropping. And we never knew when we were going to get a meal, let alone a hot one.

I did what I could to cheer the men up. I knew how to focus on what was important: being with Bob, having enough food to eat to keep me alive (although not as much as I wanted), and being able to sleep when I could. If the men would follow my example, they'd get through this war. I knew they would.

After a couple of weeks, we earned a short break. We passed through the town of Verdun, where we got hot showers, hot food, clean clothes, and even beds to sleep in. That cheered up the men to no end.

But we all knew we would have to head into battle again. The Germans were at their breaking point. They just needed a little more persuading before they surrendered. The Allies planned another assault, and the Yankee Division would be part of it no matter what.

CHAPTER 7

VICTORY!

Our mission for this new offensive was similar to the last one. The Yankee Division's job was to distract the Germans on their flank and keep them from sending reinforcements to the midsection of the front line—where the Allies planned their main attack.

Flank or midsection, we knew the Germans would do their best to hold their ground. Their ground was known as the Hindenburg Line—three long bands of trenches that stretched as far as twelve miles behind No Man's Land. The Germans had held this position since 1914, so they were dug in deep.

We were getting ready for the big push when we got

more bad news. Major General "Daddy" Edwards, who had been with the Yankee Division since we shipped out for France, was going home. Daddy always made the men believe they could take on every new challenge, that they could fight with dignity and go home at the end of the war, victorious. When the men learned he was ordered back to the States, they felt like they had been slapped in face by the top brass.

Now we were heading into our biggest fight yet without the leader the men trusted most. No one was happy.

Beginning on October 16, 1918, the men were back on active duty and getting ready for an assault on the German's flank. Between the mud, the rain, the high casualties, and the loss of Daddy, the men faltered. Spirits dipped lower and lower.

I did what I could, but honestly, I was getting tired of the war, too. I made it my main job now to keep Bob safe as he moved around the battlefield collecting intelligence.

We needed to fortify ourselves for whatever came next, and the army gave us a little time to do that. We had a short rest and a chance to get clean and eat regular meals while the Allies thought about the best strategy.

On November 1, the Allies resumed their main assault on the Hindenburg Line. We were in a better position now, and we began to gain ground. The news we got at headquarters was good—slowly at first and with too many casualties, the Allies took the first line, and then, suddenly, they were pushing on with such force that they advanced by a mile.

While that was happening, the Yankee Division continued its fight on the outer flank, called the Neptune sector. We gained ground and lost it and then gained it again. We didn't have enough men, and the ones we did have were hungry, tired, and in low spirits, but we pushed on inch by inch.

The Germans constantly sent their gas shells in our direction. Some of the chemicals made it hard to breathe, others caused temporary blindness, and still more made the men break out in painful blisters. Gas masks didn't always protect us.

On November 2, 1918, both Bob and I were caught off

guard. The shell came so fast and furious that I had barely barked a warning when it hit. We got our masks on, but not in time. Both Bob and I struggled to breathe and had to be taken to a field hospital.

It took me a few days to fully recover. It took Bob longer. While he was still in bed trying to get his strength back, I traveled around the ward, visiting men and cheering them up. I even made friends with a Red Cross nurse, and when she visited Bob's bedside with me, she realized she knew him from back home. They had a good, long talk about Connecticut and people they both knew.

Bob needed that taste of home just then, and I was really happy to be able to give it to him. It helped him to get well. Unfortunately, that also meant we were ready to head back to the battle's front lines.

We knew the war was about to end. People had been saying for a long time that Germany and the other Central powers were about to surrender, and finally they said they would. We even knew the day and time the guns would stop firing—November 11 at eleven o'clock in the morning.

That seemed silly to me. Once you decided to end a war, shouldn't you just end it? But that's not what the armies did. They kept fighting right up until the very last minute.

On November 10, we were ordered to continue our assault. No one wanted to die on the last day of the war. Some soldiers straggled behind, leaving those in front even more vulnerable.

It seemed like the big guns didn't stop firing for even one second as both the Allies and the Central powers tried to use up all their shells. The noise was deafening, throughout the day and night. And then suddenly, it stopped.

At eleven o'clock in the morning on November 11, 1918, the guns were silenced.

The silence was deafening, too, for a moment.

And then the silence was replaced by normal sounds— raindrops falling from tree leaves, a horse neighing, even the *tweet, tweet, tweet* of one brave bird who flew over No Man's Land to see what was happening.

The doughboys tried to cheer, but they were too exhausted to make a lot of noise. Some stumbled off, searching for food or a bed.

Bob dropped to his knees and pulled me into a hug. He had tears in his eyes. "It's over, Stubby," he said. "It's over."

A lot of the other guys gathered around us. They thought of me as a good luck charm. Now that the war was finally over, they wanted to clap eyes on me again to make sure I was okay, and to say thanks.

I didn't do anything for you that you didn't do for me, I thought. *But I sure do appreciate the thanks—now where's the chow?*

After the news of the armistice sunk in, the celebrations really began. Without worrying about sniper fire or shells exploding, the men were able to build bonfires to warm themselves up and to dry out their wet clothes. Some doughboys even made their way into No Man's Land to trade military souvenirs with their German counterparts.

I made a trip into No Man's Land myself, followed by

the medics. We were searching for wounded soldiers we might still be able to help. Unfortunately, all we found were bodies to bury.

That night, while colorful signal flares arced across the sky, the men had lots of unanswered questions. The biggest and most often asked was, "When will we get to go home?"

But for now, we mostly just celebrated the peace.

It wasn't until later that we learned that our last battle—the Meuse-Argonne Offensive—was one of the deadliest battles in American history. It lasted forty-seven days: from September 26 to November 11, 1918. More than ninety-five thousand men were wounded and more than twenty-six thousand died.

John Curtin, the sergeant I woke up to make him put his gas mask on, was one of the Yankee Division's survivors. I'm proud to say he wrote a poem about me called "Our Regimental Mascot":

Listen to me and I will tell,
Of a dog who went all through hell,

With the 102nd infantry, U.S.A.
Stubby was with us, night and day.

He was smuggled across the sea,
And, certainly was full of glee,
When he landed at St. Nazaire,
He and Bob were a happy pair.

Near Neufchateau he stayed a while,
And in hiking, covered many a mile,
Then in February we left for the front,
And Stubby was ready to do his stunt.

A month and a half on Chemin des Dames,
Stubby behaved just like a lamb,
Then he went to Beaumont in Toul,
And Stubby showed he was no fool.

He always knew when to duck the shells,
And buried his nose at the first gas smells,

But once a small fragment stuck in his breast,

Slightly wounded in action, was Stubby blessed.

He went all through Chateau Thierry drive,

And came out of it very much alive,

Then to St. Mihiel Stubby came,

And helped those Germans from the plain.

North of Verdun were our hardest battles,

And many brave men gave death rattles,

But Stubby came through hell O.K.

And is ready to go back to the U.S.A.

He is a fighting bulldog of the old Y.D.,

And is the pride and joy of our company,

When we take him back to the U.S.A.,

Stubby will hold the stage night and day.

His owner Bob will take him home,

And nevermore will Stubby roam,

He'll enjoy a much earned rest,

In the place we all love best.

He stood up to read it at a victory celebration and the men whistled and cheered and clapped. Then they sang, "For He's a Jolly Good Fellow" to me!

Happy to help, guys! I barked. *Happy to help!*

Bob couldn't wait to go home. I didn't remember much about Connecticut, but I was ready to go anywhere he went.

"You're coming home with me, Stubby," Bob said. "If I have to, I'll sneak you on a ship like I did before."

I go where you go, I told him. *I'm yours, and you're mine.*

But we couldn't go home yet. We were needed to stay in place to keep the peace. The men hadn't slept in days; they hadn't showered in weeks. Their uniforms were caked with mud. Six hundred men at a time traveled to Verdun for twelve-hour leaves that included showers, hot food, and fresh clothes.

Finally, on November 14, we were relieved of our

peacekeeping duty and could leave the trenches behind forever.

Au revoir, *rats! I hope I never see any of you again.*

We marched for eight days—more than a hundred miles—to a relief camp in Montigny-le-Roi, where we had to wait out the peace negotiations and make sure the cease-fire stayed in place.

By the time it was all over, we had served 193 days on the front lines and participated in seventeen battles.

We were assigned to civilian houses, and the French people were happy to let us stay with them. We had been at war for a year and a half, but they had been under German fire for over four years.

For the first time since our visit to Paris, Bob got a real bed to sleep in—which meant I did, too. Clean, dry sheets beat the mud in the trenches, that's for sure.

While we waited for orders to go stateside, men we hadn't seen in a long time started to arrive to rejoin the unit—Yankee Division guys who had been wounded and ended up fighting with other divisions when they got out of the hospital. Even men who had been taken prisoner by the Germans started to come back. They all had stories to tell.

I had stories of my own. One of the best happened on Christmas Day, 1918. President Woodrow Wilson paid a visit to the Yankee Division. The 102nd Infantry greeted the president and the first lady at the train station. Then there was a review of the troops on a parade ground and a Christmas dinner with the officers.

Finally, when the president was on his way back to the train station, he stopped to talk to some of the doughboys—including Bob. And that's when he met me!

Bob saluted, and then I did. And all those people with the president clapped for me.

Then the president reached his hand out, and I shook it. I shook paws with the president of the United States!

If a stray dog from the back alleys of New Haven, Connecticut, can help win a world war and shake hands with the president, then anything is possible.

CHAPTER 8

PEACE

While the men waited for news about when they would be shipped home, they began to collect medals. There were US victory medals, French medals for bravery, and medals and ribbons for individual battles. Bob pinned most of his to my jacket. Plus, we each had a wound stripe and three gold chevrons—one for each six-month period we spent in France.

All of that hardware, plus my pawshake with the president, made me the most famous dog in France. Wherever we went, doughboys and French people wanted to say hello and get to know me.

Then newspaper reporters started nosing around and

writing stories about me for the folks back home. Soon I was the most famous dog in America, too. I wondered what that would mean when we got back home, but for now, I was happy for clean beds, lots of food, and a place by Bob's side.

In January, we got the order to leave Montigny-le-Roi and head to a camp near Le Mans. It took three days by train. We hoped we'd get the order to go home from there, but I guess the countries were still negotiating the peace. To keep boredom at bay and the men in fighting shape, we had to do drills again like we had in Connecticut. Only these were more fun—we had gas mask races and tent-pitching contests, and our five-mile hikes weren't done at the quick step.

Even better, six hundred men at a time got to go on furlough. Bob and I set off for Paris on March 13, 1919. We were going to go on a two-week tour of France, but then Bob got sick with the flu.

The flu was bad—very bad. People all over the world were dying from it. Bob had a high fever and could barely stand. He knew he needed to check in to a Red Cross hospital, but he was worried about who would take care of me while he was there.

I can't lose you now, I told him. *You go to the hospital and get well. I'll take care of myself until you're better. Don't worry.*

"Let's go together, Stubby," Bob said. "You've charmed generals and presidents. What are a few Red Cross nurses and doctors?"

It turned out that there were way too many flu victims to fit in the hospital. Only the very sickest were admitted. The rest were taken care of in tents nearby.

A pale, sweaty, and weak Bob approached the doctors and told them about me. He pointed to the medals on my coat so they could see how important I was.

I was at my most charming. I smiled up at them and then I sat down and saluted. *Let me stay with my doughboy*, I told them. *We helped win the war.*

The doctors walked a few feet away to talk things over. And this is where my far superior dog's hearing came in handy. They were trying to come up with a plan to keep Bob and me together. Then someone made a suggestion they all agreed with.

"Stubby can bunk alongside your cot in one of the hospital tents," a doctor said, coming back over to us.

"Thanks, Doc," Bob said, giving me a scratch behind the ears. "Stubby and I appreciate it."

But the doctor wasn't finished. "If your condition worsens and you need to be moved inside, then the dog won't be able to come with you."

I eyed Bob. *Don't get any worse*, I told him. *Or these doctors are going to have a lot of trouble on their hands.*

Bob didn't get worse. A cot, lots of soup, and nurses fussing around him was all he needed to get better. And, not surprisingly, I became a favorite of the staff and the patients. They wanted us to stick around until Bob had to go back to his unit, but we wanted to see more of France. So as soon as he was able, with six days left in our leave, we headed south to see the Mediterranean Sea. It looked the same as the Atlantic Ocean to me, but Bob seemed to like it.

My favorite part was the trains. We didn't travel in boxcars the way we did to the battlefields and back. We traveled in the style befitting a couple of war heroes. We sat in velvet seats and ate in the dining car.

And then we got the best news of all when we rejoined the Yankee Division. We were going home!

In late March 1919, we boarded the *Agamemnon*. There was no sneaking on board and hiding in a coal bin this time. I marched up the gangway with my head held high, and we set sail for Boston, Massachusetts.

Au revoir, *France. We're going home!*

CHAPTER 9

HOME

The ship approached Boston Harbor on the afternoon of April 7, 1919. There was a dense fog—something the doughboys had hoped to leave behind in France. When the ship sailed out of the mist and we could see the docks, boy were we surprised. Thousands of people waited to welcome the soldiers home—friends, family members, strangers, and even a few governors.

The person the Yankee Division was most excited to see was Major General Clarence "Daddy" Edwards. He may have been shipped stateside before the war was over, but most of the men gave him the credit for keeping them alive.

"Daddy! Daddy!" the men cheered.

When it was our turn to finally leave the ship, I marched down the gangplank at Bob's side, wearing all my medals. People had already heard of me from newspaper articles, and the cheers for me were almost as loud as those for Daddy.

But mostly everyone just cheered for home. Soldiers and spectators alike, everyone cheered for the good old USA.

But just because we were back on US soil, it didn't mean we could go to our real homes—not yet. It took a lot of paperwork and other human nonsense to leave the army, and so after a quick trip to see Bob's family in Connecticut, we found ourselves in yet another camp, Camp Devens, outside of Boston. Only this camp didn't have rats and lice and bullets flying. The food was always hot, too.

The men talked about home and what they were going to do there. Sometimes they marveled at what they had seen and what they had done in France, but mostly they looked to the future. It wasn't long before they, and they rest of the country, started calling the war "the War to End All Wars." I hoped that was true.

Bob and his buddies were all anxious to get home and begin their new lives. I guessed I would be starting a new life, too. I was going to miss all the guys, but I'd be with Bob and his family. Being with Bob was the most important thing.

Before the men were officially out of the army, we marched in a huge parade in Boston. I had marched in a few parades by then, but this was the biggest one yet. I trotted along next to the 102nd's color guard—the men carrying the flags. I followed the Stars and Stripes, my eyes straight ahead. Then came the order for "eyes right."

I turned to the reviewing stand where all the bigwigs sat, and then faced forward again. That got a huge response from the crowd.

I'm a trained soldier, I thought. *That's no big deal.*

That parade was our last big job as soldiers. Less than a week later, Bob was discharged. He packed his gear, and this time—unlike when he first left for France—there was no question that I was going along.

"I'm a civilian now, Stubby," he told me. "And that means you are, too. Time to go home."

Things were hectic there, too. At least at first. We marched in a couple of small parades in Connecticut, and then it was time to settle down into our new life. That's when we found out how famous I really was. Calls and letters started coming in asking me to do all kinds of crazy things. The craziest one Bob said yes to was a tour with a vaudeville company. In the middle of all the other acts— singers, comedians, actors, and dancers—I'd march onto the stage, sit down, and salute the crowd.

Unlike officers, vaudeville audiences don't salute back. So on Bob's signal, I'd drop to all fours and trot off the stage. It was an easy job, but Bob hated all the travel. We settled down in New Brighton, Connecticut, and Bob went back to his old job as a salesman.

The requests to appear kept coming. I marched in more parades, saluted at victory-bond drives to earn money for returning heroes, and even got a free lifetime membership to the YMCA with the promise of a place to sleep and three bones a day whenever I was away from home.

There were so many newspaper stories about me that Bob started a scrapbook to keep up with it all. And Boston terriers became one of the most popular kinds of dogs to adopt as pets.

I was happy in Connecticut, but I knew I'd be happy anywhere Bob was. So when he packed up and moved to Washington, DC, to go to law school, I went along. We lived with a whole bunch of other former doughboys called the Carry On Club, and got to work. While Bob was learning about the law, I was learning football! I became the mascot for Bob's school and got everyone in the stands excited about the game at halftime.

I became famous all over again, and President Warren G. Harding (who was elected in 1920) decided he wanted to meet me. So I went to the White House and shook his paw. A few years later, I would meet yet another president—Calvin Coolidge. By that time, I was starting to feel right at home in the White House.

But long before then, I met the man that Bob said was the biggest honor ever—General John J. Pershing. Pershing was the man in charge of the American Expeditionary

Force during World War I. Lots of doughboys believed that his leadership was the reason we won the war.

On July 6, 1921, Bob dressed in his best suit and made sure my coat was clean and that all my medals were shiny. We made our way to the State, War, and Navy Building in Washington, DC, and told the guards we were there to see the general.

"No dogs allowed," a guard said.

"But this is Sergeant Stubby," Bob told him. "He's expected by General Pershing."

I sat down and saluted, but I guess only officers are swayed by that trick. Finally, they made a phone call, discovered that Bob was telling the truth, and let me in.

Lots of reporters were waiting for us inside. The Humane Educations Society had created an award for me, and General Pershing was going to be the one to give it to me. The medal was solid gold and had a picture of me engraved on it.

The general made a speech about my bravery on the battlefield, and then he pinned the medal on my jacket. I bet it was the only time he honored a dog.

Since he made a speech, I thought I should, too. *It was nothing,* I barked. *I'd do anything for Bob and the rest of the doughboys. Let's just make sure we stay out of war from now on.*

Life got a little calmer after that. Bob had law school, I was busy on the football field, and we went to as many veterans' activities as we could. For about a year, Bob took a job with the Bureau of Investigation (it's called the Federal Bureau of Investigation, or the FBI, today), but he had to travel too much. I stayed with the Carry On Club whenever he was away, but neither one of us liked being apart. He resigned and settled into a government job in Washington, DC.

I kept marching in veterans' parades and raised money for the Animal Rescue League, but by 1926, my football days were over. Bob and I had been together for nine years. I didn't know how old I was for sure, but Bob guessed I was around eleven. And the truth was, I was tired. It was harder and harder to get around. I didn't even have the energy to eat more than a few bites anymore. Bob took me to a doctor, but they said there wasn't much they could do. Old age had caught up with me.

I hated to leave Bob, the best human in the world, but I could tell I was going to have to. We were at home in our Washington apartment, when I realized it was time for me to rest forever. I thought about Smitty and the other soldiers I had seen go on the battlefield.

Bob was there for me in the same way I had been there for Smitty. He cradled me in his arms. "I'm going to see you through this, Stubby," he said. "Thank you for being the best dog in the world."

I looked up at him. His thoughts mirrored by own.

"Thank you for being my closest comrade, and for keeping me alive all through the war," he added.

I tried to raise my head to lick his tears away, but I couldn't. Instead, I did my best to give him a smile.

I closed my eyes. It felt good to rest in the arms of my best friend. And then I let go.

Goodbye, my friend. Thank you for being my human.

HISTORICAL NOTE

This book is a work of fiction, but Stubby was a real dog who became the official mascot to the 102nd Infantry Regiment during World War I. Although it's impossible to know what he was really thinking and feeling, most of the events in this book really happened. Others are imagined.

James Robert "Bob" Conroy wanted future generations to remember his brave dog and to learn about Stubby's contributions in World War I. He made sure that Stubby's body and his impressive uniform were preserved. Today, you can see Stubby at the Smithsonian National Museum of American History in Washington, DC.

World War I began with the assassination of one man—Archduke Franz Ferdinand. The archduke, the heir to the throne of Austria-Hungary, and his wife, Sophie, were traveling in Bosnia, a province of Austria-Hungary. Many people in Bosnia wanted Bosnia to become a part of the Kingdom of Serbia. With the archduke's visit, they saw their chance to make a statement.

A Serbian man killed the archduke and his wife. Shortly thereafter, Austria-Hungary and its partner, Germany, declared war on Serbia. Other countries in Europe quickly chose sides.

Russia joined with Serbia and declared war on Austria-Hungary and Germany.

Germany invaded Belgium and Luxembourg on its way into France.

Great Britain, France, and Belgium joined Russia in the fight against Germany and Austria-Hungary.

Other European countries were forced to choose sides.

Eventually, the Great War, as it was then known, involved two dozen countries, including the United States. It spread to Africa, Asia, and the Middle East. It was the first war in which modern weapons were used— weapons that inflicted terrible damage. As many as twenty million people were killed.

The soldiers who survived this terrible war told themselves that surely it had to be the War to End All Wars. Then World War II broke out in 1939. The Great War, the War to End All Wars, became known as World War I.

SERGEANT STUBBY PROUDLY SHOWING OFF HIS UNIFORM ON THE WHITE HOUSE LAWN FOLLOWING A MEETING WITH PRESIDENT CALVIN COOLIDGE.

STUBBY RECEIVES A MEDAL FROM GENERAL JOHN J. "BLACKJACK" PERSHING.

STUBBY AND ROBERT CONROY SPENT A LOT OF TIME ON TRAINS IN FRANCE AND IN AMERICA AFTER THEY RETURNED HOME.

CAMP YALE IN NEW HAVEN WHERE STUBBY JOINED HIS
UNIT IN THE SUMMER OF 1917.

AT CAMP YALE, THE SOLDIERS PRACTICED MARCHING, SHOOTING,
AND STANDING GUARD, AND WERE DRILLED IN TRENCH WARFARE, AS
SHOWN HERE.

STUBBY PROUDLY SHOWS OFF HIS YANKEE DIVISION
PATCHES AND THE EMBROIDERED WREATH OF FLAGS FROM
EVERY ALLIED COUNTRY.

GAS MASKS WEREN'T JUST FOR HUMANS. THIS DOG (NOT STUBBY, BUT STILL HANDSOME) SHOWS US WHAT STUBBY WOULD HAVE LOOKED LIKE IN HIS.

A SKETCH OF SERGEANT STUBBY ON A HAND DRAWN MAP OF SOME OF THE PLACES WHERE HE FOUGHT IN FRANCE.

ROBERT CONROY AND STUBBY POSED FOR A PORTRAIT IN FRANCE AFTER THE WAR ENDED.

STUBBY WAS A POPULAR PARADE LEADER WHEN HE RETURNED HOME.

STUBBY WAS THE GUEST OF HONOR AT THE HUMANE EDUCATION SOCIETY PARADE IN MAY 1921, SERVING AS "GUARD OF HONOR" FOR MISS LOUISE JOHNSON.

FURTHER READING

Want to learn more about WWI and other military animals? Check out these great books.

Everything World War I by Karen L. Kenney with historian Edward G. Lengel, National Geographic Kids. An illustrated, fact-filled look at the weapons, the soldiers, the spies, and the countries that fought in the War to End All Wars.

G.I. Dogs: *Judy, Prisoner of War* by Laurie Calkhoven, Scholastic. The first book in the G.I. Dogs series tells the story of a dog who became an official prisoner of war on the island of Sumatra during World War II.

Military Animals by Laurie Calkhoven, Scholastic. Read about the dogs, horses, elephants, and even carrier pigeons that have aided soldiers through the ages.

Stubby The War Dog: The True Story of World War I's Bravest Dog, by Ann Bausum, National Geographic. A nonfiction account of Stubby's remarkable life.

Truce by Jim Murphy, Scholastic Press. Murphy tells the story of a Christmas truce, a day in 1914 when soldiers on both sides of the war defied their commanding officers and celebrated Christmas with their "enemies."

The War to End All Wars by Russell Freedman, Clarion Books. A comprehensive look at the conflict that spanned the globe and changed the way that wars are fought.

ABOUT THE AUTHOR

LAURIE CALKHOVEN spent her summer vacations on a farm in Iowa ruled over by a St. Bernard dog named Ginger. At home in New Jersey, Friskie (a mutt adopted from the dog pound) refused to be trained not to run into the road. Then she ran right into a moving car. Friskie got around on three legs after that and learned not to play in traffic. There's no room for a dog in the New York City apartment where Laurie currently lives, but her nieces and nephews have four: Hudson, Meisje, Molly, and Lucy. Laurie is the author of many books for young readers, including *Military Animals*; *Women Who Changed the World*; *Dog's Best Friend*; and the first book in the G.I. Dogs series, *Judy, Prisoner of War*.

Don't Miss G.I. Dogs: *Judy, Prisoner of War!*

Turn the page to read the first chapter . . .

ESCAPE FROM SINGAPORE

Singapore was under siege. As a ship's dog on the HMS *Grasshopper*, an English gunboat, my job was to keep the men's spirits up and warn them when danger was near. Today, danger was all around.

Japanese bombs had been falling since December. The first Japanese troops entered Singapore in February 1942. On the eleventh, the British got the order to evacuate. Soldiers, government workers, and British and Chinese families all crowded the pier, fighting for a place on a ship—any ship. Every vessel, from small fishing boats to private yachts and passenger steamers, no matter how old, was called into service.

Gunfire and bombs were all around us. The normal waterfront smells mingled with the unsettling scents of smoke and death. And underneath all the other smells was fear. The civilians, especially the children, were terrified, and it was my job to help them. I was afraid, too, but I never let them see it.

On February 13, the final evacuation began. Sailors desperately tried to keep order on the pier while confused and frightened mothers and children came on board the *Grasshopper*. My friend George White gave each person a cup of tea and a piece of chocolate, while I wagged my tail, nuzzled little fingers, and barked a hello.

Welcome to the Grasshopper, I told them. *You're safe here.*

As darkness fell, we began to pull out of the crowded harbor, when suddenly we got the order to turn around. There was another group of refugees who needed to come on board. Every inch of the ship was already full, but we somehow made room for more.

We finally left the harbor after midnight. The hardest thing was hearing the shouts from the people who had been left behind. I stood on the deck and howled with them.

I'm sorry. We're already dangerously overcrowded. There's no more room.

As soon as we were out of earshot, I snuggled down between two of the most frightened children and tried to get some sleep. But, as always, my ears were on alert for the sound of Japanese warplanes and the bombs they carried.

With luck, we'd make it to Java in a few days, and from there, larger ships could take us to India or Australia.

Unfortunately, luck wasn't on our side.

I'm going to tell you the story of how I became an official Japanese prisoner of war during World War II, and how I managed to keep myself and my men alive.

But before we get to all that, let's start at the beginning—in Shanghai, China.